A Note to Parents and Caregivers:

Read-it! Readers are for children who are just starting on the amazing road to reading. These beautiful books support both the acquisition of reading skills and the love of books.

 The PURPLE LEVEL presents basic topics and objects using high frequency words and simple language patterns.

 The RED LEVEL presents familiar topics using common words and repeating sentence patterns.

 The BLUE LEVEL presents new ideas using a larger vocabulary and varied sentence structure.

 The YELLOW LEVEL presents more challenging ideas, a broad vocabulary, and wide variety in sentence structure.

 The GREEN LEVEL presents more complex ideas, an extended vocabulary range, and expanded language structures.

 The ORANGE LEVEL presents a wide range of ideas and concepts using challenging vocabulary and complex language structures.

When sharing a book with your child, read in short stretches, pausing often to talk about the pictures. Have your child turn the pages and point to the pictures and familiar words. And be sure to reread favorite stories or parts of stories.

There is no right or wrong way to share books with children. Find time to read with your child, and pass on the legacy of literacy.

Adria F. Klein, Ph.D.
Professor Emeritus
California State University
San Bernardino, California

Editor: Jill Kalz
Designer: Nathan Gassman
Page Production: Melissa Kes
Associate Managing Editor: Christianne Jones
The illustrations in this book were created digitally.

Picture Window Books
5115 Excelsior Boulevard
Suite 232
Minneapolis, MN 55416
877-845-8392
www.picturewindowbooks.com

Printed in the United States of America.

Library of Congress Cataloging-in-Publication Data
Shaskan, Trisha Speed, 1973–
Marconi the wizard / by Trisha Speed Shaskan ; illustrated by
Amy Bailey Muehlenhardt.
p. cm. — (Read-it! readers)
Summary: When the young wizard Marconi magically packs his school bag every
morning, it gives him exactly what he will need, and it knows when he will need it.
ISBN-13: 978-1-4048-3167-4 (library binding)
ISBN-10: 1-4048-3167-3 (library binding)
ISBN-13: 978-1-4048-1234-5 (paperback)
ISBN-10: 1-4048-1234-2 (paperback)
[1. Wizards—Fiction. 2. Magic—Fiction.] I. Muehlenhardt, Amy Bailey, 1974– ill.
II. Title.
PZ7.S53242Mar 2006
[E]—dc22   2006027287

Marconi the Wizard

by Trisha Speed Shaskan
illustrated by Amy Bailey Muehlenhardt

Special thanks to our advisers for their expertise:

Adria F. Klein, Ph.D.
Professor Emeritus, California State University
San Bernardino, California

Susan Kesselring, M.A.
Literacy Educator
Rosemount–Apple Valley–Eagan (Minnesota) School District

PICTURE WINDOW BOOKS
Minneapolis, Minnesota

My name is Marconi, and I am a wizard. I go to Watson's Wizard School. Every morning, I use magic to pack my magical wizard sack.

5

First, I wave my wand and say, "Oh, great wand, please help me pack my magical wizard sack." I know the magic is working when a rainbow glows above the sack.

This morning, my wand packs a grape ice pop, a box of tissues, a bottle of gold glitter, a carton of orange juice, and a muffin.

8

I carry the sack on my shoulder and walk toward school. A strong, hot wind blows over me. Then I see flames coming out of a cave. The flames belong to Firebomb the Dragon.

I wave my wand and say, "Magical wizard sack, please take out what I need." The grape ice pop floats out of the sack.

"That is just what I need! My throat is on fire!" Firebomb says. "How did you know that grape is my favorite flavor?"

"I just knew," I say and toss him the ice pop.

Suddenly, I hear a loud "ACHOO! ACHOO!"
The noise is so loud I cover my ears. I see
Maddock the Giant. Then Maddock sees me.

I wave my wand and say, "Magical wizard sack, please take out what I need." The box of tissues floats out of the sack.

"That is just what I need! I have such a bad cold," Maddock says. "How did you know that lemon is my favorite scent?"

"I just knew," I say and toss him the box of tissues.

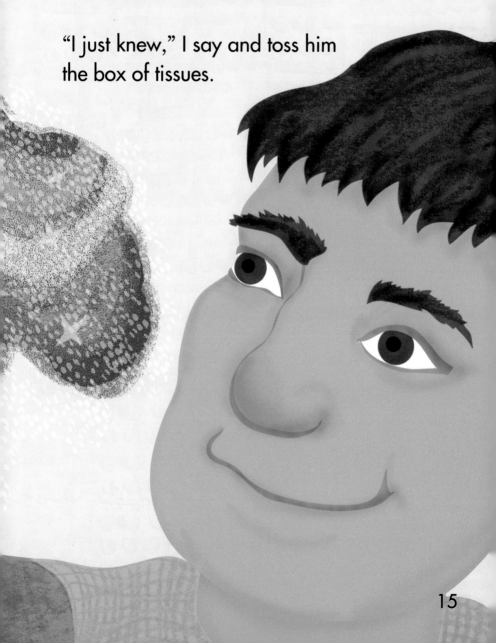

15

16

Just before I get to school, I see a stream of gold glitter hanging in the air. I follow it to a yellow tulip. Twinkle the Fairy is inside. She is crying.

I wave my wand and say, "Magical wizard sack, please take out what I need." The bottle of gold glitter floats out of the sack.

"That is just what I need! I lost the glitter on my wings and can't fly until I get more," Twinkle says. "How did you know that gold is my favorite color?"

"I just knew," I say and toss her the bottle of gold glitter.

When I get to school, I feel hungry. My stomach growls. I look all around, but I don't see anything to eat.

21

Then I smile and wave my wand. I say, "Magical wizard sack, please take out what I need." The carton of orange juice and the muffin float out of the sack. I don't ask how my favorite breakfast appears. I just know.

More *Read-it!* Readers

Bright pictures and fun stories help you practice your reading skills. Look for more books at your level.

Alex and Toolie
Another Pet
The Big Pig
Bliss, Blueberries, and the Butterfly
Camden's Game
Cass the Monkey
Charlie's Tasks
Clever Cat
Flora McQuack
Kyle's Recess
Peppy, Patch, and the Postman
Peter's Secret
Pets on Vacation
The Princess and the Tower
Theodore the Millipede
The Three Princesses
Tromso the Troll
Willie the Whale
The Zoo Band

Looking for a specific title or level? A complete list of *Read-it!* Readers is available on our Web site:
www.picturewindowbooks.com